MW00528863

LITTLE BIRDS

filthyloot.com

LITTLE BIRDS

Book & cover design by Ira Rat

FIRST EDITION

SAM PINK

NOT A TROPHY

Enemy mindset

steamrolled

and run up a flagpole.

Not a trophy

but a warning.

RED ANTS

For a second

it felt like

my blood

was maybe

many many

tiny red ants.

And it's true

even though

it's not true.

IT

When it is in your heart

the only defeat is

forgetting that

and victory is

every second of remembering.

The blade falls on your neck and becomes a necklace.

And your blood is pollen anyway.

Welcome welcome.

ELLE NASH

HIT ME BABY ONE MORE TIME

In the room, I start my show. A few people enter, chatting as usual. I pull up an app onto the screen with my goals.

200 tokens - top comes off.

500 tokens - bra comes off.

1000 tokens - vomit on cam.

Blue text materializes above me on the screen, alerting me of a few new subscribers. The sound of coins dropping into a slot machine. I turn on the tub faucet, wet my clothes, begin to peel off a pair of socks. E. calls from the kitchen. She's home early.

/

It was infectious. I had recoiled at first but the longer I thought about it, the more I wanted to go back.

Do certain words affect the body? The desire inside me ticks and ticks and ticks. In bed at night, I feel it start at the center of my forehead and move outward, a tiny pulse. I know where it is operating. A quick, light throb down to the edges of my fingertips. I am awake and then asleep again within myself. I reach out for E. and her back curls away from me like rolled paper. My mind is merely looking for something to engage it. I cannot disengage with myself.

And I prefer the internet because I don't like having a body.

/

I position myself on the rim of the tub, laptop set on toilet, seat and lid down. Dee27 asks for a private message and sends me 50 tokens.

Will you let me mod for you? Dee asks.

I'd seen the username around a fair bit. Dee had dropped a few high tips over the last few weeks. I decide to accept. On screen my face moves closer to the camera, the sound of typing, my tits.

"Dee27 is this month's mod," I tell the room. "Don't fuck with me or you'll get banned. And stop sending fucking dick emojis on chat."

More blue text. The sound of making money. Dee27 sends another message, which is how I know he's a man.

You shouldn't vomit on cam, Dee says. _You're better than that. You could be working for a studio._

"Please don't lecture me on what I should and shouldn't be doing," I type back. "I will ban you, too."

It's uncomfortable to watch.

"My comfort is absolutely more important than your freedom," I say.

The room was silent and no one had tipped in a while. A door sweeps open, the swing of keys, E.'s heels. Her voice from the hallway, calling my name.

/

I go shopping. I put things in the cart I want: two pounds of purple potatoes, some rye bread, fig bars, some fruit. I get what E. wants, which I consider the necessities: enough meat for the week, popcorn kernels, cooking oil, diet soda. I walk around putting more things in my cart. I walk up to the check out desk, then turn around. I'm doing math in my head for how much it will cost. The organic fig bars are six dollars and I know I won't keep them down so I put them back. I get kale instead. I put back the rye bread. I place the bag of purple potatoes on top of a tub of apples in the produce section.

/

I sweep up food crumbs from yesterday's dinner and see a row of ants crawling from under the sink towards the back of the fridge. The faucet pours water into the sink all over the dishes and the sink fills, clogged with food. The ants swim towards each other, grasping arms, making little ant-clumps that float along the top.

When the fans are on and the doors are closed,

the apartment is so big. Everything is far away. At night with the dark closing in and the doors open, it's all too near.

/

I open the room again on the cam site, same time every day, when E. leaves for work. The regulars, Dee, and some newcomers are on. I press my tits against the plastic container and look into the camera.

"Do you think if I tried to forcefully vomit into this bucket when it was across the room, and I missed, and we went back in time and replicated the situation precisely, that I would still miss?"

Dee responds into the chatroom. I lean in to see the response.

_I don't know what you mean. Like odds,

50/50?_ it says.

"I mean if we replicated the conditions exactly, down to the molecule, down to the position of the moon."

I'd like to think there was a possibility you could make it. Isn't there something that says we are flashing in and out of existence so quickly that it cannot be seen? Wouldn't it be somehow different? Dee says.

"But my hands are in the same positions, so is the bucket, so is everything, the vomit is the exact same weight and volume. Would I still miss?"

Someone else types into the room: _tits please._ And tips me 100 coins. "Thank you, OG Gilbert." I move the plastic container from in front of me.

Dee enters text into the chat. _I guess if everything was the same..... then yes, I think you would._

"So doesn't that imply that life is not random," I ask. "That the conditions have to be just right for this thing to happen? And if that is the case, life is predictable? But it is so infinitely complex that its predictability cannot be measured?"

I wait for a response.

"If nothing is random then free will does not exist," I say.

Randomness is a perceptual issue, Dee says. _It cannot be measured._

"But we can't go back in time. So we don't know that something is predictable. It doesn't really answer the question of free will."

You can still make a decision and change the course of your life, Dee says.

/

At what point does it stop becoming a game?

/

E. comes home smelling like the perfumes of other women. I enjoy it, not my own perfume or hers, the smell of others more novel. I am trying to remember the last time I felt truly lost in the abandon of my youth. The sound of a jet overhead. A large, empty feeling of danger. The wild eye of a cat in the dark.

My greatest sexual fantasy is she holds me down and filets the insides of my wrists open with a fish knife.

I touch her breasts, the crease of her eyelid

pulses. I breathe in, she breathes out like she's been running. My lungs dry inside like a stack of hay. We are all shopping, all of the time.

I go to sleep and dream of her. Wearing blue, feeding me coins.

The usual. I can never get to her, for whatever reason.

NATE LIPPENS

CONVICTIONS

Arlo was out of jail. He had been in and out of trouble and custody most of his teens and then he went from the kind of trouble that involved drinking and motor vehicles to the kind of trouble that involved forced entry and weapons, crossing over from criminally stupid to stupidly criminal.

I told him that if he went back to prison I wasn't visiting him. I would write him but I didn't want phone calls. I didn't want to enter all my personal information online again and set up an account with Telmate so the crooks profiting off of the crooks could exorbitantly overcharge me. He said he understood. He said he was going to meetings. He was only seeing his probation officer every six weeks for a home visit during which she showed up early or late and stood in the sparsely furnished living room of his mother's apartment and asked him rapid-fire questions about work and recovery. He said he was randomly drug-tested without fear of the results. He was doing well, thanks.

The letters arrived stamped in red: This is from a Correctional Institution. They arrived like a séance, but filled with boredom, hokery, and meandering philosophical rantings in scrawled handwriting.

"I'm writing large. I'm in the dark to some degree. You're the easiest person to write to yet I put it off. I get to a point where I don't write any more. Sometimes it's easier not to think of the outside world. Try to focus and get shit done here. It's been foggy for two days now. No movement due to visibility. If the guards can't see us, they can't shoot us."

I filled out a form with his prisoner number and handed over my I.D. Then I checked my wallet, phone, and jacket in a coin-operated locker, changed out a twenty for quarters, and took off my boots.

I passed through the metal detector and had my hand stamped like I was entering a nightclub. I crossed the yard from the guardhouse to a low brick building. The visitor room looked like a cafeteria but all the food was served from vending machines. There were assigned tables and murals of smiling families. The lighting was bright. It was a bit like a heavily guarded theme restaurant.

I watched outside and could see Arlo coming

across from the other unit. His limp was more pronounced than usual. He appeared at the door and smiled. He waited to be buzzed through and checked in at the desk.

I stood and we hugged. We made awkward chit-chat. I shook the bag of coins. “Want something to eat?”

“I’m thirsty but I should take it easy. They’ll strip search me if I use the can.”

“Drink slow.”

“That your motto now?”

“Only here. What you want to drink?”

“Diet something. I’m watching my weight.”

He laughed and smiled. There were two fading bruises on his jaw.

I wanted to ask but I knew better. These visits were a careful balancing act. The wrong subject could piss him off or quiet him into a sullen funk.

He had accused me of thinking that I was better than him. That these accusations had been made during visitation hours across cafeteria-style tables surrounded by other similar arrangements of families and friends, some talking, others sitting mutely searching for words or past the point of words, in a variety of locations with the names that end in Correctional Institute, had not helped his case, nor had it made me any less guilty and sad.

At the vending machine, I perused the selections. I was disappointed that they didn't have coffee. The previous prison had coffee and the guards were much friendlier. They also had games and cards. Neither of us played but it had appeared to make people around us happy. Less family squabbles and baby-mamas yelling.

The dress code had been more lax too. At the guardhouse here no less than five signs said skirts must be three fingers long. Somehow that was a more suggestive description than an actual measurement.

I bought us two diet sodas, cheese puffs, and red licorice whips.

"Surprised they let you have whips in here. Potential weapon."

We talked and joked. We gossiped about celebrities and TV and movies. He asked how I was and I lied. He showed me the same courtesy. We switched to a topic that never tired us: men. Men from the past. Men from the now. Men as we imagined them to be. I talked about a guy I'd been dating and he talked about a man he worked with in the kitchen.

We were running out of steam before the visiting hours were done and stumbling along. The awkwardness at our table wasn't what unsettled me. It was the silence at the other tables around us where after years of visitations there was nothing left to say.

The visit was cut short because the prison went on lockdown.

I asked one of the guards if there was any chance that if I waited in my car in the prison's parking lot that the situation would be resolved and I could resume my visit. The guard, young and nervous, said no. Not with much conviction but with the air of finality uniforms lend.

I started the trek home with a tight-knuckled

grasp on the steering wheel thinking about fairness. The absurdity of it. I heard the word as spoken by several different friends' voices. One sounding small, petulant, child-like or an approximation of a child that everyone thinks exists but doesn't. Another lined with pity: That's unfair. The friend would say it, cast her eyes down at a loose step stone, and ash her cigarette. I wouldn't tell anyone what had happened. It was part of a long line of unfairness.

As I drove, I thought about dinner, about what was in my fridge at home, about my tired drive's end and preparing a lone meal and watching TV.

Last night, I had stayed up too late watching a movie with smart dialogue and dumb violence. One punctuating the other until it became a game for me, guessing if the movie would end with a bloody scene or final words. I fell asleep before I found out.

I dreamed about one of the actors. A minor character in the movie who seemed to carry his own light, something from within showing through his eyes. That was how I had recognized him: his eyes. He had played young, fearful, teary men in police procedurals on TV. Since then he had bulked up and played hired killers and abusive boyfriends with dark childhoods shown in flashbacks.

My hands loosened on the steering wheel and I knew I wasn't going to make dinner when I got home. I saw the familiar lights of the fast food joint and pulled off. The line was long but someone pulled in behind me immediately and then I was committed to it. I anticipated the taste the salt, the sharp chemical diet soda, the way it would carry me the rest of the way home where I wouldn't call anyone and wouldn't cook. I would lie in bed and try to find that movie and stay awake long enough to watch the actor die or not die, kill or be killed, and shine.

SHANE JESSE CHRISTMASS

HAIR TONIC.

Blinds fallen from the window frame. It is late morning. Tight jeans ... muscular ... hard chest ... wax-paper wrappers around tobacco cinders. Anthony and I are in the shower room at the gymnasium. Shower spray on skin. Bony frames enclosed in perfume. My hand all scabbed. Hand previously ripped open by metal fence post. I am on my knees. I want to sleep. I want to be able to sleep. I am sick ... therefore it should be easy to be to rest. All I need to do is sit. Anthony wants me to sleep on the toilet. French Fries from McDonalds ... reading about a quadruple murder out in Poughkeepsie. Six wires inside my spine. Vaseline on my fingers. Glass pipe in Anthony's fist. Anthony says I need to get more toothpaste. He asks me if I am an addict. I say no. Anthony asks me if I would like to know what it means to be an addict. I say yes. Anthony says he is glad to hear it. I bite my lip ... my nostrils twitch. Anthony and I hug in the corner. Anthony tells me I should start eating my own skin. I eat it and spit it out. I spit it all out. My fingernails are filthy ... milk-white skin. I'm asleep on the hardwood floors ... covered in pale-blue sheets. Anthony is one weird fucker. Anthony is on the floor ... in the dark ... his fingers in my hair. His body. It is not real. He has a powerful ass. Anthony wipes his fingers on my face. His rotten armpits ... sweat inside a wine glass. Anthony wearing latex underwear ... sipping on coconut rum. Anthony walks to the window ... his eyes are shining. There is no need to open the window ... but he does. A voice ... fire burning. Anthony hears something. He runs his hand down my chest. He smiles. Late autumn morning. The wind is gentle ... cold enough. My shoes are made from scraps from an old shoe factory. Anthony is in the bathroom playing with the shoes. We tumble to the ground. My eyelids. I'm in the bathroom ... I turn the water on. The bathroom's empty. I find a towel and put it over Anthony's feet. I'm wearing earmuffs ... heading to the liquor store ... to get more bottlecaps. Anthony pulls me close. It is cold. Blade bent and turned ... inside my right thumb. Blood dripped from the wound. I knew I must have bled once. Sun-burnt wallpaper peels onto the laundry tiles. My skin flakes into the laundry basket. Anthony has just got a new tattoo. It's scabrous. He's surprised ... says it will end up mighty fine. He's collecting bottlecaps. Is Anthony trying to eat my flesh? What has been in my mouth? Nothing. My hands tied in knots. Grief in the air. Anger and sadness and grief in the air. A few minutes pass. Then something stirs inside of Anthony. Anthony says I may have a high exposure to hypnosis. I go to the convenience store. I purchase soap and toothpaste ... some deodorant ... facial creams ... several boxes of tissues. He's lying on his belly ... he's crying. I have a lot of scars on my neck. I go to the gas station. I buy some gas. I want to get a tire. I want to put a tire in a van and pay the gas station a hundred dollars. I want to drive the van to the gas station to take the tire to the gas station. Anthony's legs are twisted ... I go to shower. I need to get my hair done. My hands are tied in knots. My hair sticks to my forehead. I can get rid of the hair later ... but I need to go get my eyes cleaned. Scars from a lot of cuts. They're a lot easier to cover when I'm sleeping. I'm going to make a couple of changes to my hair. Anthony uses his ass to make others feel powerless and helpless.

I might use some hair tonic. Jumper cables for the car battery. I need to purchase some. I do not have to have to feel the pressure that is getting applied to my brain. Anthony says he cannot be stopped. I do not have to be afraid. I do not have to be held down and pushed. Anthony says he might become a Baptist. I call bullshit on that. Fungal spores on Anthony's foreskin. My eyes are open ... I am staring straight ahead. Anthony says it is creepy. My legs straighten out. I am on the floor. Anthony's blood on my clothing. He is in my bathroom. I've pulled my clothes together. I do the dishes. I wash my arms and legs. I do the dishes. I turn off the stove. I turn off the stove. I do the dishes. Anthony's blood on my clothes. I have cleaned him. He's all clean and ready to go. I am in the car. I pull up to a gas station. I ask Anthony if he needs extra fuel. Meth in exchange for meat products.

BRIAN ALAN ELLIS

Sext: Reject me harder

Text received from co-worker:

Are you okay?

responds to text with long, heartfelt confession about not being okay

Text received from same co-worker:

Can you switch shifts with me at work tomorrow?

Dude, Where's My Serotonin?

Q: What if reincarnation was real and we were destined to live an infinite amount of lives?

A: Then I would definitely fuck up each and every one of them.

♫ My cries for help bring everyone else's cries for help to the yard ♫

Me:

I can't cope. I am miserable. What do I do?

The Internet:

There are situations in your life too ridiculously painful and humiliating to share but they must be shared. Go on, my child, share them.

Externally, internally—find a screamer who does both

Q: What's new with you?

A: Oh, nothing I haven't already regrettably overshared on the Internet.

sues self for emotional damages

Me:

I deserve better.

My inner voice:

Ummm actually....

Humans being turned into computers wouldn't be so bad, just as long as those human computers had decent Wi-Fi

Computer:

You don't have the latest version of Office.

Me:

True.

And I also don't have an actual bed.

Or any furniture.

At all.

G.C. MCKAY

CHAMELEON

I was standing in a queue lined up in sets of twos or threes, but I stood alone. A fling from the past had got in touch, most likely on a multiple gamble of male names, and told me to come down to the same shithole club we first met at, stating she was already there, and that she wanted to see me. What with our recent history and my supposed (or in her mind, assumed) want of getting some action, I'd asked a friend at the bar we were at if he wanted to come along. He frowned, appalled by my suggestion. After getting snubbed again by a couple of other friends via text messages, I decided, half against my better instincts and half overruled by my subconscious, to scheme alone, and take things in my stride from there.

As I paced towards my destination with a

determined, yet oblique reasoning, I could sense something else entirely had brought me back to that place. It seems I'm akin to a fly that keeps going back to the same spot, no matter how many times you bat it away. Since this feeling struck me as something beyond the scope of my own understanding—*or beyond the scope of human understanding entirely*—it'd be an act of futility to try and describe it in a manner I'd ever deem satisfactory. But what I will say, for better or worse, is that I felt a certain alignment with a metaphysical mechanism, an atomisation of myself. Put simply, only half of my actions were my own, and some uncaring force was driving me forward towards a dishonest, though of course, perfectly natural encounter.

The Flying Mantis. The neon sign, underneath which I stood, camouflaging those who dressed in red. It was your typical student bar back before it was shut down, with drinks as cheap as the thrills its clientele were on the hunt for. And that was exactly what made the place so palatable to the tongue. You didn't have to hold onto your morals so tightly in there.

But that was before a certain rumour spread, during the indefinite period the club spent with its doors closed. Nobody seemed to know when it was first shut down or when it sprang back up, but the club had re-opened as if nothing had ever occurred there. As if leaving it locked up and alone with the breaths of the past circulating between its blackened walls would somehow erase the tarnished reputation it now possessed.

The longer I ponder this idea, the more I've come to believe that the new, unwashed reputation it carried was exactly the reason many a person returned. Though whether any of them realised that or not would be pure speculation on my part.

And I can only speak for myself.

The club was nearly shut down for good because the previous owner used to prey on young women who frequented there. He'd get all friendly with a certain type; the (preferably) drunk, feather-brained and-slash-or cognitively lacking ones who could only spot a snake after they'd been seized and squeezed by one, and usually still struggle even then. After he'd slipped a Rohypnol... or *'planted one of his roaches,'* as he so often stressed... into one of the drinks that just kept right on coming, he'd lead them into the back... somewhere dark I imagine, to encourage their blackout, and wait; somewhere near the stairs which led to the ladies' room. Trusting all went well and none of the girl's friends were around to intervene, he'd throw on his hero's cape and carry the unconscious girl in question to his office, where she could *'get a grip of herself'* and he could *'call the authorities,'* if and when need be.

He never said an ambulance.

Only ever the authorities.

After raping them he'd come out of his office and start bawling about how the girl might be in some serious trouble, playing the victim to spite his latest one. His trick was to shove his own fingers down the girl's throat so that her body's survival instincts would kick in and wake her up—*mid-puke yet post-raped*—whereby the time her consciousness realigned itself she'd find herself already covered in her own bile. She wouldn't really be awake, but more half-conscious, with no idea what was going on, dilapidated by the stench of her insides. If her adrenaline was cruel enough to wake her up sober, the owner still had the upper hand, for he was the sole possessor of the single set of keys to the door. The door to an already soundproofed room, further isolated by the penetrative music that pumped against the ceiling. The door to a room, which only contained a singular, frosted window that was only transparent around its bordered edges, trusting one stood and peered in from the most acute of angles...

Mmm. I've only just realised that I was thinking about that same story whilst waiting in line to get inside The Flying Mantis, for the first time since it'd been closed. And now is the first time I've come to realise that they didn't even bother renaming the place after all the events that'd taken place there.

Perhaps there really is no such thing as bad publicity.

"ID please mate," said the bouncer. Somewhat

snapped out of my wild imaginings and without protest, I flipped open my wallet. Without looking, he glanced to the left and to the right of me, where I noticed his eyes worked separately from each other as opposed to as one. Whilst appearing to look over both of my shoulders at the same time, he queried, "Here on your own tonight?"

"Yeah?" I said, unintentionally adding the inflection of a question, and momentarily perplexed as to why.

"You're the first bloke I've ever seen turn up here by himself."

Some guy and girl behind me laughed, which provoked a delighted, if not somewhat forced chuckle out of the bouncer in front of me, providing him with an unwarranted thrust of confidence for the modest price of my humiliation.

"There's a first time for everything," I replied,

once again unsure of my speech's cadence; of my own meaning.

"Not if I don't let you in there won't be."

I paused here and looked beyond the bouncer's gait to find myself focusing on a couple of girls who were walking up the street. Both wore skin-tight cocktail dresses with nothing else but a couple of leather handbags barely big enough to hold their purses. Just looking at them during that brief interlude seemed to make the chill in the air grow harsher, causing my ears to burn and turn red.

"Watch yourself," the bouncer's tongue slowly snapped, as if he'd been observing the reflection of my focus and didn't know what to make of my glare. He waved me in without saying another word but trailed my movements as I ambled through the two-way double-doors.

I went up the narrow staircase, encased

by the thumping music thudding against the poster-sheathed walls. All of those advertisements were obsolete, though a few of their scratch marks somehow appeared to me as new. For a brief moment, I considered getting rid of my jacket as I passed the cloakroom, but since the price of entry was double that of hanging your coat, I decided against shedding my second skin for the time being. I liked the idea of looking like I might be on the move at any second anyway, and, to be honest, the look gave me more sexual agency than if I were to go in without it.

£3 and a couple of permanent marker stains of vermillion across the back of my hand later, I was inside the joint. Instead of looking for Hedda (the girl I was there for), I headed straight to the bar. It stretched across most of the left-hand side after you strode past the toilets, with a couple of barriers to put your drinks down around a metre or so to the right, where beyond that at the centre was the forever humidified dancefloor. To this day, I cannot remember a single evening of ever taking a step onto that circular hunting ground without feeling like I was walking over the fresh crime scene of a previous conquest.

Sobriety wasn't doing me any favours at all inside that place alone, so I ordered a couple of cleaning-product looking shots along with a double vodka and red bull, necking them all before 'remembering' to also get myself a pint to wash away the coat of chemicals across my palette. The girl serving me, who had tightly pulled-back braids of lightning peroxide blonde and a deliciously pissed off face freckled about the nose, seemed to enjoy my obvious *need* for a drink, until some other prick literally snapped her back into subservience...

and our moment of speculative tension sunk like the shots she'd only just served me.

Upon turning, the harsh light of the bar swirled with my sightline as I instinctively started looking around the beat-pumping cave for a pretty face, half-wondering to myself whether I should even bother acknowledging the girl I was supposed to meet there. But as my eyes realigned, my points of focus failed to detect her. Something in my saliva, however, could taste her in the air.

Hedda and I had already hooked up a couple of times and even gone out on what I suppose you could call a date. All were hardly the most stimulating experiences of my life. I suppose something about her intrigued me, or maybe I thought it did due to a lack of options and an abundance of self-inflicted isolation, but during one particular so-called date, she seemed a lot more interested in her fucking phone than with... well, anything else. This was before mobiles turned into our entire world as well, so in a way, I had more of a right to be pissed off about such a thing, from a historical point of view. Notwithstanding the question of etiquette. Nowadays the usage of phones is so commonplace that to even question the teeny-tiny hit of vacuous, undeserved and slow-dripped dopamine people get from their mindless, self-orientated filters and status updates is to mark yourself an out of the times philistine and backward threat to the groupthink mentality. The arrogance of the herd deserves to be raped with the utmost aplomb.

Sometimes I feel like a fly, observing a mosaic of persons from the outside looking in whilst on the inside looking out, able to pull back, on occasion, and witness the sight as one to see that these supposed persons are all one and the same... all at the same one time as well. Ignorance of this glaring algorithmic nightmare must be a blessing indeed. I can feel its cleansing quality even now as I suck the thought through my teeth.

Unfortunately, the alcohol was taking its sweet time to kick in that night, and the haze before me, assumedly from some smoke machine, seemed to serve as a place to hide for the surrounding animals. As I wandered through the wilderness, their faces snarled and eyes shone with something perniciously arcane, and therefore terrifying. *Never ever enter a nightclub sober again*, was my loudest thought as the terrible music beat through my body against my will. For a moment, it felt like it was my heartbeat, dullened and monotonous, pumping for no good reason at all except for the sake of pumping. The voices around me would've almost been comical if it weren't for their quality of alienation. I wasn't sure if it was all eyes on me, or whether I was simply sensing their observation of my presence through my own eyes somehow... as if I were, for a brief period, experiencing both viewpoints in parallel.

I lit a smoke on a pivot turn and was about to head to the bar again, but a hand with several metallic rings on it flew out in front of my face and trapped my cigarette, relinquishing it from my possession; once again, against my approval. Shuffling back to where I was just standing, Hedda, the girl in question, eventually came into view.

My initial thought: *fat.*

It must've been longer than I remembered since we'd last seen each other. Three months, maybe longer. When we first met, she was probably a ten. Now she was pushing a good fourteen or maybe even sixteen. Can't say it looked all that bad on her, but bigger girls have never really been my preference.

Then came my second impression: *arrogant*.

Ten or so weeks previously, Hedda had shunned me for some other guy. She even did it inside the very club we were currently standing in, right in front of my eyes. I couldn't quite believe a girl that average could rustle up a harem of men for herself. But now the guy she really pined for had most likely fucked her off after fucking her. She must've been eating for comfort ever since, and now lucky old me was in for a slice of over-puffed, sloppy Swedish pie.

"Nice to see you," she said, sucking away on my cigarette with a flirtatious and all-too-at-ease look on her face, playing it dainty and cute, which curdled my testosterone beyond awful.

"Hey," I half-yelled back, then pointed at the bar.

She nodded. As I paced forward, her arm entwined with my own. That was the moment I should've said something, should've let her have it with words instead of action. My body practically jolted with disgust at her presumptuous nature. However, looking back at it from certain angles, I can see how she was probably embarrassed by her previous behaviour with me and was trying to make light of it to put us on an even keel. But she was acting like a girlfriend... acting as if nothing had ever happened between us... and latched herself onto me like I actually meant something to her. If only she'd said sorry for behaving like such a sack of shit. I guess saying it is just too much for most people. Even for me... or so it may seem.

At the bar, I bought myself an additional couple

of shots and another pint. Hedda looked a little stunned to see me neck them both without even bothering to look at her, let alone offer her one, but she awkwardly laughed it off and ordered herself some sparkly pink-looking concoction; a gin that glittered called Unicorn Tears, at which I guffawed upon first sight. As she took a ladylike sip, I observed her for the first time that night. I liked the way her lips looked as they sat perched over the rim of the glass, her eyes puffing out as she sucked down the alcohol she'd need for what I had in store for her. The drink appeared to blend with her lipstick as well... which in turn woke her cheeks into a delicate flush. Her white dress, though obviously not all that complimentary, did have a pleasing, subtle pattern to it as well. Under the garish, neon light of the bar, I could see a bubbly texture of fluctuating infinitesimal lumps.

My mouth suddenly became parched as I trailed the pattern to the hem of her left sleeve, where it appeared to continue over her bare skin. Her goosebumps provoked me into sucking in the dry sweat across my teeth, where a seething sound rattled inside the cave of my mouth. Hedda, to both my surprise and chagrin, kissed me out of nowhere, lathering her tongue across mine in a sandpaper scratch. For some reason, I thought of picking at a scab when you know you shouldn't, partly because it feels good, partly because it doesn't, just for the satisfaction of drawing blood. I caressed Hedda's cheek down to her collarbone, then ran each finger across the edge of her dress, feeling how it clung to her body like a thickening second skin, imagining how delicately, or perhaps how violently, I'd have to peel it off during our mating ritual.

The girl at the bar, for some reason, seemed to

be orbiting within our realm. As she served us, the flickered glances daggering between Hedda and I were more than palpable, but I couldn't tell if she was on her side or mine. It was as if she were confused by our being together, that something about us didn't quite match up, like we were to be feared because our motivations toward one another were obtuse and unknown, almost like nature itself. The barmaid, sensing my registration of her observing us, walked away after sniggering at the manner Hedda sipped on her infantile-looking drink. I, in return, sneered with delight.

To be honest though, I too was getting a little annoyed with how pathetic Hedda was acting. There was a childish mannerism about her that particular evening, but instead of conveying a vulnerability I was invited to nurture and comfort, it provoked nothing in me but the deepest sense of disdain. I would've likely been blind to this had she not kept me in the back pocket of a pair of pants she most likely couldn't fit into anymore, slumped on her bedroom floor in the shape of a constricting snake. But she had left me there, quite literally, standing alone inside the club whilst she scurried off with another man, with no idea of what a man such as myself is really capable of.

Hell may indeed have no wrath like a woman scorned, but hell always has, and will always be, strictly a man's domain.

After a few more petite sippy-cup sips of her acidic-looking excuse for a drink, Hedda excused herself for the bathroom. It hit me then that she was also alone inside the club. I figured she'd come along with friends, since normally there was at least one other female lurking around her aura from time to time, and usually that person, for some reason, could never quite look me in the eye. This night though, nobody was around; and yet, for some unknowable reason, I couldn't help but feel the strongest sense of being watched. The static in the air seemed to be aware of my presence.

The girl at the bar was staring again. She was absentmindedly wiping back and forth along the counter, in rhythm to the ticking of a clock that was nowhere to be seen. As I returned her glare in a shifting blink, her sightline jolted away from mine in a reflex of a feline. I took a heavy gulp of my drink, marvelling how the alcohol felt as it quenched the sudden aridness of my being. Without giving it much further thought, I sunk the rest of my beer and slammed it down on the nearest coaster, then picked up a stranger's and necked it as well. The sudden need to piss came as no surprise. As I made my way through the faceless crowd, half of me hoped Hedda would be gone by the time I returned. And yet still, to this day, I cannot reconcile myself with the reason why.

I saw her just before entering the toilet, sucked into the fluorescent vacuum of her phone. Her eyes sat on a plateau between glee and unbearable grief, as if the dopamine provided by the other end of her screen was already waning, and the desperation for a bigger dose was more than demonstratively portrayed by the jittery manner of her tenterhook fingers. She was standing outside the office of ill repute I was talking about earlier, oblivious to the horrors that were once carried out there. Or just indifferent. Grazing her shoulder as I passed, her body flinched electric, but her neck made no jerk towards its cause, according to the peripheral of my right eye anyway. I entered the toilet without looking back, with the scent of Hedda's over-sprayed, commonplace fragrance erecting the hairs of my nostrils, only to have them assaulted and burned alive by the stench of poorly aimed-at metallic toilet basins and crumbling urinal cakes.

My teeth were still sweating somewhat, so I lit a cigarette as I pissed to counter the repugnancy of my environment. Mid-stream, the eroding pipes above my head gave a sudden, gargling wail, feminine in nature, licentious by design. The voice of a woman whose word is not worth the air into which it is uttered.

The previous owner of the club got caught when one of his victims committed suicide. Nobody knows what really happened, but certain rumours circulate with an air which seems to ring truer than most, or which appeals more to the palette of our collective, guttural consciousness. The usual method of operation had been employed by the club owner, which had proved successful for close to three years up until this point. But something must've gone wrong somewhere. Perhaps his dealer gave him a dud dose; the girl in question could've also been on a number of narcotics that could've easily countered the effect—but I guess we'll never quite know for sure.

My favourite rumour strikes a chord within me that screams with a want to ascertain its validity, though of course, I know better than to believe it simply because of that. I forget the original source, since I mostly pieced it together as if I were a collector—*or perhaps even hunter of sorts*—casting my net over a host of scattered whispers and impulsive musings, each one of them flaking; shedding themselves into particles beyond interpretation, with nothing left to identify them but the original degree of excitement buried within the expected and (what I suspect) largely forced intonations of shock and horror when the incident was first spoken of in a hush.

Our rape victim was already wasted, garish in her behaviour and as unstable in her mind as she was on her feet. Our hero—*for if you were there, this was the role he'd most likely convince you he was playing*—stepped up to his familiar sporting ground, probably in utter disbelief of his luck. Hell, he might have thought that he didn't even need to *roach* the girl. Food tastes better when it's free, so why wouldn't rape? Maybe that's where he went wrong. Once you get good at something, it can be easy to slack off every now and then. Overconfidence can have a tendency to slap one hard in the face, as when nature does when we collectively ignore her cries. I like to think that he felt like a fraud though. Surely the true rapist doesn't require such an obvious crutch. He could've thought himself an imposter and just that tiny slither of doubt was enough to make him decline and fall.

It makes you wonder how many traumas are only screamed in silence, whilst still knowing they hold the overwhelmingly gargantuan majority.

I suppose the hardest part was keeping the eyes of others away from that girl, that particular night. She wore her recklessness with an equal amount of abandon. Hearsay informed me part of her head had been recently shaved, and that her tattoo sleeves, covered in a blend of creatures orange and green or turquoise and crimson, all saurian, were only a week or so old... that she'd thrown away her student loan on getting over half of her body inked. Every mood she could ever possibly feel was now conveyed by the venom of her skin. An amalgamation of all to represent none. Most would probably say that on the inside she was hiding something from herself, but I'm convinced of the exact opposite: inside she was already dead, hence why her body now served as a shrine to everything she once ever felt.

They say that a tattoo should signify an important event in your life.

How many, do you think, signify what somebody is trying to hide?

Eye shadow for the unexplained insomnia.

Concealer for the revealing blemish.

Tattoo for the identifying trauma.

Everything... everything can make sense outside the spectrum of human emotions, if and when looked at with the same unlawful apathy of the life force we're nothing but at the mercy of...

The girl then danced, bumping into the backs

of strangers with her hands in the air. Her tears sat inside her eyes in a constant state of convulsion to expose what was really going on inside her mind, an onslaught of thoughts that stabbed and sliced and eviscerated themselves so they could never be understood. A sacrifice of neurological patterns, with their tripwires forever triggered. During one stumbling moment, the prince of the hour stepped in and caught her mid-fall, which some people seem to think might've been staged somehow, a way for him to win her over on first sight. He escorted her away from the dancefloor, a few heads watching, giving him a nod of recognition to his apparent nobility, with what would later be discovered to be a group of men who were already in the know when it came to his antics.

I sometimes wonder which is worse: being the rapist and carrying out the act... or knowing a rapist and allowing him to carry it out.

A person's silence really does say an awful lot about them.

As planned, our prince exited the dancefloor with the blacked-out girl quite literally draped over his arms, eyes rolling around the back of her chemical-kamikaze of a head, tongue flopped out of her mouth, drooling, utterly oblivious to the time and place she was in, and, somewhat blessedly unaware of the actual trouble she'd just tossed her body into. Things continued as expected inside the club, and nobody, not a single person from any of the rumours I've heard, knew anything about how the club owner had managed to get the girl inside his office without any fuss. I guess here is where the story becomes a form of conjecture and speculation. One report floated around stating that some lonesome male was standing around outside the club owner's office, somewhat inconspicuously peeking through the transparent inch of glass that bordered the otherwise out of focus pane. As the rape continued and everybody inside the club took very little notice of this solitary individual, he, much like the man carrying out the rape, gained confidence in watching it being committed. I'm not sure how far that particular rumour spread, but I wonder, if it is indeed true... when he watches it back in his mind's eye, does it playback as if someone else were watching him as he stood there, alone, observing the rape through the looking glass? Could seeing that shift your memory into a third-person perspective? After all, permitting yourself to view a peepshow one should surely not bear witness to must—*without doubt*—create a crisis of identity. Which do you believe yourself to be: the monitor or the monitored, or the monitored viewpoint of the monitor itself?

CCTV is quite an obvious enemy of any rapist, and all the ones inside the club were simply there for show, to add a cruel sense of security to a very insecure situation for many a woman. It's a wonder how the place ever re-opened again, when you really stop to think about it. Then again... what's the use of four walls unless it's for sin?

So anyway, the girl woke up during the ordeal. She was being taken from behind with her body slumped across an armchair, with one hand being held behind her back. I assume this was done to add an air of believability to the rape, a way for the guy to think he was actually either fucking or raping her whilst she was conscious, but I could be off the mark. This is where I believe the trauma she was trying to hide through drink and drugs reared its ugly head inside an exact repeat of the act. She wasn't ready to confront it, hence the self-blurring of the event through narcotics and impulsive tattoos–though that, of course, is just a theory.

"Argh," the girl said, letting out a slight air of discomfort, but keeping her eyes closed all the same. The guy hesitated for a second, but then began to pump the girl even harder. Maybe he convinced himself it was a moment of genuine pleasure for her, that in this modern age it was better to be fucked unconscious anyway, when your waking life consists of nothing but the observation of ever-escalating suffering.

Forcing her arm upwards a touch, the club owner barely lasted a minute longer. As he orgasmed, no emotion appeared to be felt, except maybe that of a mild repulsion, either for the girl or for himself, or possibly a combination of both, as if he saw for a moment how he'd been led by the blindness he had in regard to himself. Believing her to be asleep afterwards, since the guy lifted her head up by her hair and she ever so cleverly played dead, allowing her body to flop so convincingly that she really did appear to be out cold, the guy left her there and vacated the room into what looked like a small, walk-in cupboard. Part of his ritual, perhaps? Nobody knows, but the man was clearly preoccupied with his thoughts. I doubt those of shame or remorse, but one never knows. He'd not only unbuckled his belt before forcing himself on the girl in question, but also removed it entirely. My guess is, he did that so that the buckle itself didn't distract him with its rattling and pose a threat of awakening the girl to the ordeal her body was close approaching. A few seconds after the door to the cupboard was closed, the girl shot up, spine as rigid as I've ever seen on a person, like she'd been thrust upwards by a surge of unique adrenaline.

The only time anyone ever looked at me like that was during elementary school. That girl, who later went on to kill herself as well via an out of control drug habit, was being molested by her uncle, who apparently was ever so insistent on looking after the little girl, every Friday and sometimes Saturday night, for close to three years before anyone considered his actions to be a little bit on the side of an anomaly. Just like then, I saw something screaming in this girl's eyes, something you know they'll never come back from. For even to imagine the helplessness of a child can be enough to cripple someone for a lifetime. Once you're exposed, whether through participation or observation, a part of you dies, and its wither of atoms linger around whatever's left of you for the rest of your days.

Without blinking, the post-raped woman snatched at the belt as if it held the reflex capabilities of a lizard's tongue as it snatched the life out of its prey. I still don't quite know how she did it so quickly, but as she approached the window, eyes determined and black according to my recollection, she managed to wrap the necessary part of the belt around her neck and use the doorknob to strengthen its grip to a level of lethal in next to no time at all. As I looked down at her and she up at me, no other assistance was needed. The girl jerked a touch from the instinctual imperative to breathe, but for the most and impressive part, she committed a clean and noble suicide.

I like to think she wouldn't have been able to

do it without me, but I guess... I'll never know for sure.

Vomit spewed out of my throat upon this thought, tearing my larynx with acidity, burning like the luminous yellow that'd fired out of my urethra only a few only moments before, which still burned even as I spat the remaining bile away from numbed lips. The smell of urinal cakes did nothing to disguise the rancid stench.

How long I spent inside the bathroom, I've no earthly idea.

All is decaying.

All is rot.

For the sake of a cause, we know not what.

I laughed as I read that, not because of the so-called poem but because I was thinking that I should go and find Hedda, only to see another scribbled contribution to the back of the toilet door:

Hedda is a no-good fucking slut!

Seemed kind of superfluous to underline the slut part but well, each to their own. I guess if I were in Sweden, I'd have probably not even given the comment a second thought, but how many Hedda's could've been living in my city? Could it'd have possibly been written by the very guy I thought Hedda chucked me aside for, or maybe the one before me, who got tossed into the gutter like a used condom after I showed up on the scene?

As soon as I vacated the toilet, Hedda confronted me. "There you are. I have been looking for you everywhere. Where have you been? I thought you disappeared for one moment there."

"In a way, I did."

"What?"

"You took too long in the bathroom, so I

went as well."

"Why did you come all the way down here? There's a men's room next to the one upstairs."

"Less people down here. More privacy," I replied, staring through the window of what was once a private office, despite it still being painted over with sloppy streaks of black.

"Are you okay?"

"Yeah. I'm fine. Just a little drunk."

"You don't seem drunk to me."

Here I paused, then jokingly added, "And how the fuck would you know what I'm like when I'm drunk?"

"I... don't know. Happier?"

I laughed, widening my eyes chaotically as I looked at Hedda. Somewhat surprisingly, she appeared to accept whatever claim I was making with only the slightest degree of hesitancy crossing her brow, nothing of which she'd dare to mention out loud. "Shall we go now?" she asked.

"Hedda's horny," I said, making a light joke out of an apathetic use of alliteration.

Hedda's eyes gleamed, quite literally, almost on the verge of excitable tears. She grabbed a chunk of my jacket and launched herself at me, utterly convinced that my announcement of fact determined my want of fucking her.

"You wanna go to yours or mine?" she asked, hooking her arm through mine, the appropriateness of which I found questionable at best.

"Neither," I said.

A small noise betrayed her, indicating a desire to ask me another question, but yet again, she kept her mouth shut, so off towards the exit we went, almost like we were an actual couple to the unknown eye. As that thought crossed my mind,

I could feel a certain smirk inside my lips that I had the fortunate stoicism not to betray.

All I remember when it comes to leaving was the look the shit-testing bouncer gave me when he saw who I was exiting the club with. Though I can't be sure if his rallying, unaligned eyes were being judgmental or not, it was, without doubt, more than palpable enough to be felt. And felt it, I did. I suppose what irked me at the time was that he had no idea of the situation, of my relationship to Hedda, or of just about any goddamn fucking thing else. He assumed (like—*and I stress*–I am now) some element of influence Hedda had over me, simply because she was the female and I the male, which really told me everything I needed to know about his psychological relationship with women. Reminding myself of this helped me stay focused and emotionally withdrawn, so ironically, maybe the next time I see him—if I ever do—I should shake him by the hand.

As we stepped onto the bus, Hedda aggravated my already edgy mood by not only allowing but outrightly expecting me to pay for the tickets home. It was all in the air of her manner, a self-gifted glimmer of female privilege that she evidently felt was within her right. I figured she was annoyed by my antics at the bar and fancied asserting herself into the position of power between us. I paid, eager to encourage this false sense of self-proclaimed sovereignty, knowing with a stern, calculated coldness that she wouldn't even get to see the front door of my house.

I knew this in my blood rather than my conscious mind as Hedda and I got off, finding ourselves alone from all angles as we crossed the main road towards the one that led to mine.

Hedda was walking slightly ahead of me... when some sudden surge of foreign adrenaline gave me the impulse to run, away from myself more than her. Where this came from, I couldn't tell you, but I could envision the upcoming sex and the inevitable, awkward moments of the morning after, and so part of me was already looking around for alternatives.

If I failed to find one, I would've fled.

As fortune (or maybe misfortune) would have it, there was some construction work going on at the church down the road from my house near the bottom of the hill. As I scanned the area for a space of relative secrecy, it occurred to me that I had been inside that church during my infant years, despite not remembering a single thing about it. I simply knew rather than recalled. Then I saw it, and guffawed, sickeningly surprised by how perfect it seemed—considering it was a portable toilet. I guess it must've had something to do with the rancid direction my thoughts were leading me, but a portaloo (as we call them here in the UK) appeared to me like the garden of Eden Hedda thoroughly deserved.

"Let's go," I said. Grabbing Hedda's arm, I led her towards our too-cramped love nest. As we approached its door, however, she pulled out in front of me and spun around to yank me inside, kicking the door open with her heel and then shut after wrapping her right leg around my hip. Her eagerness disgusted me somewhat, but the unmistakable fog of her cunt as her tongue pressed against mine soon had me in a state of frenzied arousal. Sensing this, Hedda rubbed her hand hard over my crotch. After pulling my belt loose with despicable ease and clawing my pants down a bit,

I felt the head of my cock welcome itself into the open and bitter, faecal-particle stained air. Hedda then sat down, but instead of opening wide as my cock was pointedly expecting, she began to rummage through her handbag instead. From an unknown light source through the slit of the door, I saw the shimmering foil wrapper of a condom; a multicoloured edition of a brand I was unfamiliar with, that appeared to change its tones depending on the angle of which it was held. Hedda looked up at me and gestured for me to take it. I stared at her until she slanted her head a touch. The whole time she glared back up at me with her tongue poking out of her awaiting mouth, which hung growingly agape. Ignoring the condom, I planted my left hand over her skull and thrust my rage into her mouth. At first, her gulp of shock blended with my sudden feral disposition, only to be w further by the putrid stench of our plastic, claustrophobic cave. However, Hedda forced our blinding lust into a state of dissonance before it had even properly begun. Whilst gagging through what I believe was mostly pretension, she repeatedly slapped the condom against my chest whilst occasionally abandoning her task to catch her breath, with her eyes, drool and mascara sheening in a trick of the light. This annoyed me for many a reason, but the main one was that she'd never even brought up the usage of condoms until this particular night, which only seemed to strengthen my suspicion that she'd been especially promiscuous of late. Why her sexual health was suddenly so important to her not only irked me, but also aroused me to a point of delirium that physically pricked every fibre of my being.

Not knowing why only made me want to fuck

her all the more.

By this point I was barely even looking at Hedda. My vision seemed to tunnel into a strange vignette bereft of all focus, bar the occasional widened eye. Once I'd sloppily wrapped myself with latex, I pulled Hedda up. After the repetition of going through the same motions as when we first entered the plastic shitter, I removed enough of her clothing until they no longer served as an obstacle to her cunt. Hedda settled herself into a 'just take me' position, with her hands propping her up slightly, pressing against the plastic walls with the occasional, popped-back swooping sound that makes you feel queasy and drugged.

A minute or so, or perhaps thirty seconds later, I pulled out, bored senseless by Hedda's gasps and moans, and slid the condom clean off, then tossed it at the back of her head. She turned to see that

I was just jacking off instead of bothering to fuck her. With the unspent condom plastered to her head, she seemed to take offence to witness how I was more satisfied with my own hand, and so got down on her knees.

What followed was simply a series of constant gagging, streams of saliva and smudged stains of mascara on her part, and a desperate urge to finish on mine. I treated her mouth like a gutter for the bile inside me, as my body convulsed with self-hatred and tears shook out from my blurred perspective. It was as if I were shedding myself of all the people I could've become, grieving for their helplessness as my orgasm eradicated them from my potential.

I looked at Hedda for quite a long time afterwards, breath heavy and somewhat forced. Never before have I felt so stiff yet ready to pounce at the slightest movement. On occasion, she attempted to move and clean herself up, but every time she did, I simply tutted, and she would stop with immediacy. As translucent drops fell from her chin like tears of contrition, I swept the whips of semen across her face towards and then into her mouth. As I finished up, she sucked hard on my forefinger for a long while, as if for comfort more than anything else. During this childish display, my urge to urinate suddenly grew very strong. Using my middle and forefinger as a clamp of sorts, I slowly pried her lips apart until her mouth was wide open again, with her trembling tongue seemingly in the know of my next move. I must've pissed into her mouth for longer than I'd penetrated her. What surprised me most was how second nature it appeared to be for Hedda, so much so that it almost seemed expected. It only lasted for a brief period, but I'm more than positive I'll never experience that level of intimacy with another again. That impression revealed itself as I shook and flicked the remaining drops over her nose, which caused a heaving sensation inside my chest like no other before, countered only by the emergence of vomit at the back of my throat. Zipping myself back up, I turned, then exited the portaloo, slamming the door behind me in the erroneous belief that Hedda would understand the reason its execution carried such capricious violence.

She didn't. But since part of me knew that she wouldn't anyway, seeing that I'd arguably just and quite literally thrust her into a state of frenzied vulnerability, I circumvented her inevitable chasing of me by fleeing across the road. I'm still not sure whether she saw me or not, but I definitely heard her calling my name just as I ducked behind a long line of cars to camouflage myself; her humiliated isolation echoing underneath the machinery's underbelly.

In the background somewhere a police siren wailed. Hedda kept looking left and right, even behind her own shoulder. Once she finally clocked that I'd just become a missing person in her life, her hands flopped against her sides, again childlike and pathetic. It made me gulp to see her burst into sudden, howling tears. Treating somebody like that had left a funny taste in my mouth. I yearned to go over there, almost like I was an entirely different person from the one who had more or less assaulted her only a few moments prior, but the shame that impulse brought when I considered how she'd treated me shunned my nurturing side into a wreck of meek indecision.

Despite how ill I felt, I was glad to see that she was in pain.

Suddenly, though maybe it only seemed sudden because of the emotions I was experiencing, Hedda began to cross the road. In a panic and somewhat seething fear, the last thing I wanted her to do was look at me. So, I quite literally hit the deck and wriggled myself commando-style under the car in front. When she reached the other side, she stood in the exact same position that I'd been occupying only a few seconds before. Some part of her, maybe an instinctual, ancient part of our species before we were even close to inventing language, *knew* my presence had not been entirely relinquished. Her feet shuffled. She lit a cigarette. Then I heard the seal-up button of her handbag pop open and I just knew, straight away, that she was going to take out her fucking phone, as if by memory of association.

Thankfully, her restless sighs and groans provided a good shield for any movement I'd make, so I managed to crawl myself to the other side of the car and achieve liberty. As fortune would have it, my phone actually was ringing at the time, indefinitely in fact, but I'd had the foresight to put the phone on complete silent mode somewhere back at the club. No sound. No vibration. Nothing but silence. The part that freaks me out about it, though? No matter how hard I try to recollect the moment of doing this on my phone, there exists no memory of it that I can consciously get my hands on.

Staying low, I decided to make a quick run for it. The gravel from the road proved too difficult to navigate without it alerting Hedda to my whereabouts. I'd tried moving very slowly, but this only made Hedda begin to call out my name again. She knew I was there, but something stopped her from actively looking around for me. As I darted away, Hedda's cries lost all hope, and inside the reflections of car windows, I saw the outlined blur of my body, hunched and blackened and nothing, a jittering reflex of impulsive movements beyond all my control.

After twenty or so seconds of this, I stopped running but continued walking at a fairly strong pace, my breath escaping me in long, unknowable streams. The urge to urinate had become rather strong again too, but seeing I'd nearly reached home prevented me from simply relieving myself somewhere on the street.

Naturally, I wanted to enjoy the burning sensation my urine had recently been subjected to in relative privacy. I desired nothing more than to pass my irritating waste whilst fantasising that Hedda would never show any symptoms at all.

The following morning, as I rose my fork of scrambled eggs toward my mouth, a fly happened to land on the dash of ketchup I'd coupled it with. For the briefest of moments, I could've sworn that that fly saw every single shade of all the non-entity personas I've become.

I ate it as one as if by instinct.

Brian Alan Ellis runs House of Vlad Press, and is the author of several books, including Sad Laughter (Civil Coping Mechanisms, 2018). His writing has appeared at Juked, Hobart, Monkeybicycle, Heavy Feather Review, Electric Literature, Vol. 1 Brooklyn, Fanzine, and HTMLGIANT. He lives in Florida.

Shane Jesse Christmass is the author of the novels, Xerox Over Manhattan (Apocalypse Party, 2019), Belfie Hell (Inside The Castle, 2018), Yeezus In Furs (Dostoyevsky Wannabe, 2018), Napalm Recipe: Volume One (Dostoyevsky Wannabe, 2017), Police Force As A Corrupt Breeze (Dostoyevsky Wannabe, 2016) and Acid Shottas (The Ledatape Organisation, 2014).

He was a member of the band Mattress Grave and is currently a member in Snake Milker.

An archive of his writing/artwork/music/social media can be found at: linktr.ee/sjxsjc

G.C. McKay is the author of Heather, Fubar and Sauced up, Scarred and at Sleaze. He resides in the overpriced shithole of Brighton but lives in the nightmare of cyberspace. You can find him on YouTube.

Nate Lippens is a writer and artist from Wisconsin. His fiction has been published by Catapult, Hobart, and New World Writing, and is forthcoming in the anthology Pathetic Literature, edited by Eileen Myles (Grove, 2022).

Elle Nash is the author of the novel Animals Eat Each Other (Dzanc Books), and the short story collection, Nudes,(SF/LD Books). Her short stories and essays appear in Guernica, The Nervous Breakdown, Literary Hub, The Fanzine, Volume 1 Brooklyn, New York Tyrant and elsewhere. She is a founding editor of Witch Craft Magazine and a fiction editor at both Hobart Pulp and Expat Literary Journal. She runs a biannual workshop called Textures. You can find her on Twitter @saderotica.

Sam Pink cuts you up and leaves you in the woods.

Ira Rat would like to thank everybody for their involvement and patience during this project. The process from idea to reality took a little over 2 years. It honestly means a lot to me to finally see this thing completed.